ALICE'S
ADVENTURES IN
WONDERLAND

Library of Congress Cataloging-in-Publication Data

Hitchner, Earle.
    Alice's adventures in Wonderland / by Lewis Carroll; retold by
Earle Hitchner; illustrated by Kathryn A. Couri.
      p.   cm.—(Troll illustrated classics)
    Summary: A little girl falls down a rabbit hole and discovers a
world of nonsensical and amusing characters.
    ISBN 0-8167-1861-X (lib. bdg.)   ISBN 0-8167-1862-8 (pbk.)
    [1. Fantasy.]   I. Couri, Kathryn A., ill. II. Carroll, Lewis,
1832-1898. Alice's adventures in wonderland. III. Title.
PZ7.H6296Al 1990
[Fic]—dc20   89-33889

ALICE'S ADVENTURES IN WONDERLAND

LEWIS CARROLL

Retold by
Earle Hitchner

Illustrated by
Kathryn A. Couri

Troll Associates

Alice could barely keep her eyes open. She was lying near her older sister on the riverbank. The wind was calm and the weather sunny and warm. It was all so peaceful. Alice felt herself slipping into sleep when suddenly a White Rabbit scampered by. He had pink eyes and was wearing a coat. What's more, he spoke! "Oh, dear! Oh, dear!" said the White Rabbit as he hurried away. "I shall be too late!"

A Rabbit who talks? wondered Alice. And who wears a coat? When she saw the Rabbit pull a watch out of his pocket, Alice knew this was no ordinary bunny. She got up and ran after him. Across the field she chased the Rabbit until he popped down a large hole under a hedge. Alice never stopped—she went down the hole after him.

The rabbit hole was like a tunnel sloping downward. Then, in the shadows, Alice felt the ground vanish beneath her feet. She was falling through the air!

Either the hole was very deep or she was falling very slowly, for Alice had time to look around her. The sides of the hole were lined with bookshelves and cupboards. How odd! thought Alice. Why, there are even jars of jam here! She took one, but found it was empty. Alice replaced it on a shelf lower down. She didn't want to hurt anyone who might be standing below.

Down, down, down she fell. Would the fall *never* end? Why, I must be getting close to the center of the earth! thought Alice. I wonder if I'll fall *through* the earth. Then what would become of me?

Thump! Alice fell on top of a pile of dry leaves and sticks. The fall was over at last, and she wasn't hurt. In front of her was another long passage. The White Rabbit was still in sight, racing down it. Quickly brushing herself off, Alice chased after the Rabbit again. She could hear him muttering, ''Oh, my ears and whiskers! How late it's getting!'' Then the Rabbit turned a corner and disappeared from view.

When Alice got there, the White Rabbit was nowhere to be found. She was now in a long, low hall lit by a row of lamps hanging from the ceiling. All around the hall were closed doors. Alice tried one, then two, then all of them. They were locked. How will I ever get out of here if I can't open a single door? she wondered sadly.

A three-legged table made of solid glass caught her eye. On the table was a golden key. Alice picked the key up and tried it in all the locks. No luck! But close by the floor and near a corner was a small curtain she hadn't seen before. Alice pushed it aside, revealing a tiny door. She put the golden key in the lock and turned it. *Click!* It worked!

When she opened the door, Alice saw that it led into a small passage no bigger than a rat hole. She crouched down and peered through the passage. At the other end was one of the loveliest gardens Alice had ever seen. She wanted more than anything to go there. But she couldn't get her head through the doorway. Even if I *could* get my head through, Alice reasoned, it would be of little use without my shoulders.

Sadly, Alice stood up. Then she noticed a small bottle on the glass table. That's strange! thought Alice. I know it wasn't there earlier! Tied around the bottle's neck was a paper label that had just two words printed on it: DRINK ME. She put the golden key back on the table and lifted the bottle in her hands.

Alice knew it wasn't wise to drink anything without first checking if it was safe to do so. But she could find no poison markings on the bottle. Deciding it was all right to drink, Alice uncorked the bottle and tasted its contents. It had a mixed flavor of cherry, custard, pineapple, roast turkey, toffee, and hot buttered toast. Still, it tasted sweet, and she swallowed all of it.

Alice started to feel strange. Before she knew it, she was looking *up* at the glass table. Why, she was now only ten inches tall! Alice smiled. Now she could get through the doorway.

Alice walked over and tried opening the door behind the curtain. It was locked! And the golden key was on the glass table—far too high for her to reach! Alice tried to shimmy up one of the table legs. But she'd get only a few inches up before she'd slide right back down again. She sat on the floor and began to cry.

Alice cried and cried until she became angry at herself for crying at all. Wiping the tears from her cheeks, Alice saw a little glass box lying under the table. In the box was a very small cake with the words EAT ME written in sweet icing. "Well," said Alice to herself, "I'll just eat it then! If it makes me grow larger, I'll be able to get the key. And if it makes me grow smaller, I'll crawl right under the door. I don't care which happens!"

Alice picked up the cake and nibbled at it. "Which way? Which way?" she mumbled to herself. She held her hand on top of her head to feel which way she would grow. But Alice couldn't feel any difference, and so she finished off the cake.

Alice looked down. "That's curious!" she uttered in surprise. She couldn't see her feet. "Oh, my! I wonder who will put on your shoes and socks for you, poor feet?" Alice was still looking down when her head struck the ceiling. Looking up, she realized she was now nine feet tall!

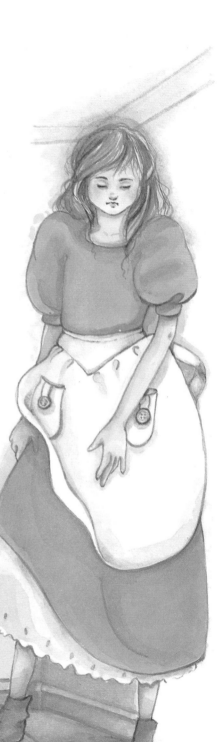

Not wasting a second, Alice took the key from the glass table and unlocked the door behind the curtain. But now she was far too big to pass through. Alice put the key back on the table and started to cry again. Huge teardrops fell on the floor. Soon there was a pool of water four inches deep that reached halfway down the hall.

Alice heard a tiny pattering of feet in the distance. It was the White Rabbit! He was coming back. And he was dressed splendidly. The Rabbit held a pair of white gloves in one hand and a fan in the other. As he trotted along, he was talking to himself. "The Duchess! The Duchess! Oh, *won't* she be angry if I've kept her waiting!"

Alice was desperate and cried out to him. "If you please, Mr. Rabbit, could you— " But the Rabbit, startled by her voice, dropped his gloves and fan and scurried away as fast as he could.

Alone once more, Alice reached down and picked up the gloves and fan. The air was very warm, so Alice began fanning herself. What a day this has been! she thought. Yesterday, everything was normal. But today, everything is—what? She couldn't quite say. She wasn't even sure if *she* was normal now.

As she thought about all this, Alice was amazed to find that she could put on the Rabbit's white gloves without any problem. How could I have done that? she wondered. I must be growing small again! Alice walked over by the table. Judging from its height, she guessed she was about two feet tall. But Alice was still shrinking. Immediately, she dropped the fan that was causing her to shrink—just in time to save herself from shrinking away to nothing.

"Whew!" said Alice. "That was a close call!"

She hurried over to the door. But it had swung shut and was locked again. And the key was back on top of the table. Once more, Alice was too small to reach for it. She was now smaller and sadder than ever. "What more could possibly happen to me?" she shouted out to no one. At that moment, Alice slipped. She was up to her chin in salt water. She had fallen into the tears she had cried!

Alice tried to keep afloat. The idea that she could drown in her own tears upset her greatly. But then she heard a splashing sound in the water. She swam closer to where the noise came from. It was a mouse, no bigger than herself. He must have fallen in just as she had.

Keeping her chin above water, Alice called out to him. "Mr. Mouse! Do you know the way out of this pool of water?" The Mouse paid no attention to her. Alice asked again. "Mr. Mouse, could we please have a chat?"

At this, the Mouse lurched out of the water and quivered with fear. "A cat?" cried the Mouse, still shaking. "Did you say 'cat'?" The Mouse looked around as if he expected one to lunge at him at any moment.

"No, no," said Alice. "I said 'chat.' Could we have a *chat*. Not *cat*. I know you don't like cats."

"Not like cats!" fumed the Mouse. "Would *you* like cats if you were me? Well?"

"Perhaps not," replied Alice in a soothing voice. "Yet I wish you could meet Dinah. She's my cat back home. She's such a dear thing. Dinah purrs and licks her paws and fur clean and is very good at catching mice—oh, I beg your pardon! We won't talk about her anymore if you'd rather not."

"*We* indeed!" said the Mouse testily. "As if *I* would talk about such nasty, low, vulgar things as cats! Really! Don't let me hear you say that name again!"

"Oh, I won't, Mr. Mouse," said Alice. Then she decided to change the subject. "How about dogs? Do you like dogs? There's such a nice dog near our house. It'll fetch things when you throw them. It'll sit up and beg, too. Why, the farmer who owns it says the dog can kill more rats than—oh, dear, I've done it again!"

The Mouse was now swimming furiously away from Alice. Water churned as he paddled.

"Please come back, Mr. Mouse!" Alice called out. "I promise we won't talk about cats and dogs since you don't like them."

"Let's get to shore," called back the Mouse, "and I'll tell you why I hate cats and dogs. Besides, it's getting rather crowded in here."

The Mouse was right. The pool of water was now filled with all kinds of creatures who must have fallen in, too. Among them were a Duck, a Dodo, a Parrot, and a Baby Eagle.

Alice, the Mouse, and the rest of the animals swam to shore. They were all dripping wet.

"The best way to get dry," said the Dodo, "is to run a caucus race."

"What's a caucus race?" asked Alice.

"Why, the best way to explain it is to do it!" replied the Dodo. The other creatures nodded in agreement.

They all lined up and ran around in a sort of circle. They ran when they liked, and they paused when they liked. After half an hour of running, the Dodo suddenly shouted, "The race is over!" They all stopped and crowded around each other, asking, "But who won? Who won?"

The Dodo thought about this question for a long time. Then he said, "Everybody has won, and all must have prizes!"

"But who is to give the prizes?" asked the Parrot.

"Why, *she* is, of course!" said the Dodo, pointing at Alice.

The whole party crowded around her, calling out excitedly, "Prizes! Prizes! We want our prizes!"

Alice didn't know what to do. Then she had an idea. She reached into her pocket and pulled out a small box of candies. Opening it, Alice handed each animal a candy as a prize. There was exactly one piece of candy for each of them.

"But she must have a prize, too, you know," said the Mouse, happily munching on his candy.

"Of course," said the Dodo. Then he looked at Alice. "What else have you got in your pocket?"

"Only a thimble," said Alice sadly.

"Hand it over here," said the Dodo. Alice did as she was told. Then the Dodo took the thimble and said, "We beg you accept this fine thimble as your prize." When he finished, all the other animals cheered.

Alice thought the whole thing was crazy. But because she didn't want to hurt their feelings, Alice curtsied and accepted the thimble from the Dodo's hand.

"Mr. Mouse," she said, staring at him, "you promised you'd tell me why you hate, you know, C and D."

"Oh, mine is a long and sad tale!" began the Mouse with a sigh.

"It *is* a long tail, to be sure," said Alice, looking down at the Mouse's tail. "But why do you call it sad?"

The Mouse ignored her question and started his story again. But he had hardly gotten a few words out when he noticed Alice wasn't paying attention to him. "What *are* you thinking of?"

"I'm sorry, Mr. Mouse," said Alice. "Please go on. I could tell you had come to a bend in your story."

"I had *not*!" cried the Mouse angrily.

"Oh, so it was a knot rather than a bend," said Alice eagerly. "Please let me help you untie your knot!"

"I shall do nothing of the sort!" shot back the Mouse. "You insult me by talking such nonsense!"

"I didn't mean it, Mr. Mouse," pleaded Alice. "But you're so easily insulted, you know."

"*Ugh!*" said the Mouse, clearly frustrated. "I give up!" And he stalked away.

"Please come back and finish your story, Mr. Mouse," Alice called out after him. The other animals wanted to hear it, too. "Yes, please do!" they all shouted after him. But the Mouse kept on walking.

"My Dinah could bring him back," said Alice. "Oh, if only she were here with me."

"And who is this Dinah?" asked the Parrot.

"Dinah's my cat," replied Alice. "And she's just about the best there is! Why, she can catch mice in a flash. And you should see her chase after birds. She could eat a little bird as soon as look at it!"

Instantly, the Dodo, the Parrot, and the Baby Eagle flew off. The Duck wasn't far behind them. Alice was alone once more. "I guess Dinah wouldn't be very popular down here," she muttered to herself. "I better keep quiet about her."

From a distance came a pattering of feet. Alice hoped it was the Mouse returning to finish his story. Then she heard someone talking. "The Duchess! The Duchess! Oh, my dear paws! Oh, my fur and whiskers! She'll have me beheaded. Where *could* I have dropped my gloves and fan, I wonder?" It was the White Rabbit!

Alice searched around her for the gloves and fan. But she must have lost them in the water. The Rabbit saw Alice as she was hunting about. He called out to her, "Why, Mary Ann, what *are* you doing out here? Run home this instant, and fetch me another pair of gloves and a fan. Quick now!"

Alice was so surprised by the Rabbit's command that she headed in the direction he was pointing. Alice assumed the Rabbit had mistaken her for his housemaid.

After a while, Alice came before a neat little house tucked near some woods. On the door of the house was a bright brass plate with the name W. RABBIT etched on it.

Alice knocked, but there was no answer. She then opened the door and entered. Inside was a pleasant, tidy room. And in the light of the window was a table with a few pairs of white gloves and some fans on it. Alice picked up a fan and a pair of gloves. She was just about to leave when she saw a bottle. The label on it said DRINK ME. Well, thought Alice, maybe this will make me tall again. Alice uncorked the bottle and started drinking.

But before she had drunk half its contents, she hit her head against the ceiling. Stooping to avoid breaking her neck, she let go of the bottle. ''That's quite enough, I should say,'' mumbled Alice, crouching lower as she grew taller. Soon she had to kneel on the floor. After a few more minutes, Alice was forced to lie on her side. But still she grew larger. In desperation, she put one arm out of the window and one foot up the chimney. ''Oh, dear. What will become of me now?'' she asked.

Finally, the effects of the drink wore off. Alice stopped getting bigger. But she was still much too big to get out of the house. ''It was a lot nicer at home where I wasn't always growing larger and smaller,'' Alice said with a sigh. ''And no rabbits or mice ever bossed me around there either.''

A voice rose up from outside. "Mary Ann! Mary Ann!" said the voice. "Fetch me my gloves and fan this moment!" It was the White Rabbit again. Alice felt something push against her elbow. The Rabbit was trying to open the door. After a few grunts, the White Rabbit said, "I'll go around and use the window." But when the Rabbit saw that the window was also blocked, he became very annoyed. "Pat! Pat! Where *are* you?"

Seconds later, another voice answered, "Right over here, Yer Honor."

"What's that sticking out of my window, Pat?" asked the Rabbit sternly.

"Looks to be an arm, Yer Honor," answered Pat.

"An arm? Why, who ever saw an arm that size? It fills the whole window!"

"It does indeed, Yer Honor," said Pat. "But it's an arm just the same."

"Well, it's got no business being there. Take it away!"

Alice heard what sounded like a ladder being propped against the house. Then she heard footsteps overhead. Suddenly, she felt something touch her foot in the chimney. Thinking it might be a rat, Alice gave a sharp kick upward.

"*Aiyeeeeee!*" someone bellowed. Then someone else said, "There goes Bill!" Alice had no idea who Bill was. "Catch him before he hits the hedge!" another voice shouted. "A drink! Get him a drink! Slowly now. You don't want to choke him!" Alice pieced enough bits of conversation together to realize she must have booted poor Bill out of the chimney. This was confirmed when Bill himself sputtered, "Wha—What happened? All I remember is that I was climbing down the chimney, then *wham!* Something hits me like a jack-in-the-box, and up I go like a rocket!"

The voices grew fainter, almost as if they were all whispering among themselves. Then, a shower of tiny pebbles came rattling in through the window. Some hit Alice in the face. Looking down at the pebbles on the floor, Alice saw they were really tiny cakes. "*Hmm,*" she said to herself, "I might as well eat one of them. I can't see how it could possibly make me bigger than I already am." Alice pinched a cake between her thumb and forefinger, dropped it into her mouth, and swallowed.

To her delight, Alice began to shrink. When she was small enough to get through the door, she raced outside. There, huddled together, were the White Rabbit and two guinea pigs holding up a lizard who was sipping from a bottle. Alice guessed the lizard was the unlucky Bill, lately hurled through space by her foot. All at once, the animals rushed at her, and Alice barely made it into the safety of the surrounding woods.

Once she knew the others were no longer chasing her, Alice slowed to a walk. She didn't know where she was. But she was determined to do two things. One was to grow to her normal size again. The other was to find a way into that lovely garden she saw earlier through the door behind the curtain.

Tiring from her walk in the woods, Alice stopped and leaned against a buttercup to catch her breath. Nearby was a large mushroom. But it was like no other mushroom Alice had ever seen. This one had smoke curling up from it!

Alice moved closer to the mushroom to get a better look. Raising herself up on tiptoe, she peered over the top. Alice couldn't believe her eyes. A big blue Caterpillar was sitting on top of the mushroom. His arms were folded, and he was smoking an odd-looking pipe.

"Whoooo are yoooou?" drawled the Caterpillar. Thick rings of smoke billowed from his mouth as he spoke.

Meeting a Caterpillar who both smoked and talked had Alice briefly tongue-tied. "I—I hardly know, sir," she said. "I mean, I know who I was when I got up this morning. But I think I must have changed several times since then."

"What?" asked the Caterpillar, taking the pipe away from his mouth. "Explain yourself!"

"I can't explain myself, sir, because I'm *not* myself, you see."

"No, I don't see," said the Caterpillar.

"Oh, I don't really know how to explain it, sir," said Alice. "Being many different sizes in a day is very confusing."

"It is not!" the Caterpillar snapped at Alice.

"Perhaps you haven't found it so yet," said Alice. "But someday you'll turn into a butterfly. I should think that will feel a little odd, don't you?"

"Not at all," said the Caterpillar.

"Well, it would certainly feel very odd to *me.*"

"You!" said the Caterpillar with a sneer, taking a puff from his pipe. "Whoooo are yoooou?"

Alice coughed as the smoke clouded her face. She was no better off now than when she started this conversation.

"I think you ought to tell me who *you* are first," said Alice, suddenly bold.

"Why?" asked the Caterpillar.

At this point, Alice had had enough. She angrily turned away and started walking. But the Caterpillar called after her. "Wait! Come back! I've something important to tell you." Alice did as she was instructed.

"Keep your temper," said the Caterpillar.

"Is that all?" asked Alice. Her voice was shrill.

"No," replied the Caterpillar. "So you think you've changed, do you?"

"I know I have," answered Alice. "I hardly keep the same size for ten minutes at a time!"

"*Hmm,*" said the Caterpillar. Smoke escaped from the corners of his mouth. "What size do you want to be?"

"I'd like to be at least a *little* larger, sir," replied Alice. "I mean, look at me! Three inches is such an awful height to be."

"*What?*" exploded the Caterpillar, nearly dropping his pipe. "Three inches happens to be a very good height indeed!" The Caterpillar reared straight up. He was exactly three inches tall.

"Oh, please," said Alice, "I can't get used to it!"

"You will," said the Caterpillar. "You will." He went right on smoking. After a minute or so, however, he took the pipe out of his mouth, yawned, and crawled down. As he moved into the grass, the Caterpillar said, "One side will make you grow taller. The other side will make you grow smaller."

"One side of *what?* The other side of *what?*" asked Alice.

"The mushroom!" replied the Caterpillar, disappearing into the grass.

Because the mushroom was round, Alice couldn't tell one side from the other. Finally, she reached her arms around the mushroom and broke off a bit in each hand. "Which should I try first?" Alice asked herself. Shrugging her shoulders, she nibbled on the mushroom bit in her right hand. Before she could draw her next breath, Alice felt a violent blow underneath her chin. It had struck her foot!

Afraid that she'd shrink to the size of a dust speck, Alice nibbled on the piece of mushroom in her left hand. She had trouble chewing it, so tightly pressed was her jaw against her shoe. But she managed to chew and swallow the left-hand morsel of mushroom.

"Ah, my head's free of my foot at last!" exclaimed Alice joyfully. But when she looked down, she couldn't see her shoulders. All Alice could see was an immense length of neck—*her* neck. It rose like a stalk from below.

"What can all that green stuff be?" Alice asked herself, still peering down. Then, she recognized what it was— treetops. She had grown so tall—at least, her neck had— that her head was well above the uppermost leaves of the trees. What's more, Alice could bend her neck any number of ways—up, down, sideways. Why, it was almost like a . . . a . . .

"Snake!" A Pigeon had flown by, screaming. "Snake!" he screamed again.

"I am not a snake!" huffed Alice. She was insulted.

"Snake, I say again!" repeated the Pigeon.

"Will you please stop saying that! I already told you, I am not a snake. I'm a . . . I'm a . . ."

"Well?" screamed the Pigeon at her. "What *are* you?"

"I'm a little girl!" answered Alice proudly.

"A likely story!" said the Pigeon. "I've seen a good many little girls in my time. But none ever had a neck like yours. No, no! You're a snake, all right. Next thing you'll be telling me is that you never tasted an egg!"

''I *have* tasted eggs,'' said Alice. ''Little girls eat eggs almost as much as snakes do, you know.''

''I don't believe it,'' said the Pigeon, angrily flapping his wings. ''You're after my eggs. Admit it! What does it matter to me if you're a little girl or a snake? Egg stealer!''

''It matters a good deal to me,'' Alice said sharply. ''And I *don't* want your silly old eggs.''

''Well, then, be off!'' said the Pigeon, flying down to his nest of eggs in the trees.

Alice would have been happy to oblige the Pigeon immediately. But first she had to get down to a smaller size. Twisting her neck downward into the tangle of trees, Alice looked for her hands. She still had a piece of mushroom in each. When she spotted her hands in some lower branches, Alice moved her head closer. Nibbling on one mushroom bit, then the other, she succeeded in bringing herself down to her normal size—neck and all.

That's better, thought Alice, smiling. Now that she was her old size again, Alice felt more confident about finding the lovely garden. She walked swiftly ahead, determined to let nothing get in her way. But then, something did. It was a house four feet high. And from it came the most frightful noise!

Alice took a tiny bite of the mushroom bit in her right hand. She shrank to nine inches in height, just about right for approaching the small house. Alice was trying to decide whether to go right up and knock when an odd-looking creature rushed out of the woods and knocked on the front door. He had powdered, curly hair and a face like a fish's. And when the door opened, he was greeted by a creature with the same kind of hair but a face like a frog's. From the clothes on each, Alice assumed they were servants.

"For the Duchess," said the Fish Servant, taking out a scroll and handing it to the Frog Servant. "An invitation from the Queen to play croquet."

They bowed to each other. But their hair snagged together. "*Ouch!*" shrieked the Frog Servant. "*Ow!*" said the Fish Servant. They were having a hard time untangling themselves. Alice started to laugh. Clasping both hands over her mouth, she ran into the woods so that neither servant would hear her.

When she stopped laughing, Alice walked back toward the house. Only the Frog Servant was still there, sitting by the door and staring at the sky. Alice walked right by him and knocked on the front door.

"There's no use in knocking," said the Frog Servant wearily. "First, because I'm on the same side as you. Second, because they're making such a racket inside, no one can hear you."

He was right. The noise inside—howling, sneezing, crashing, yelling—was deafening. Alice was trying to figure out a way to make herself known when the door suddenly swung open. Alice just barely ducked under a plate skimming through the air. The door shut just as abruptly.

Because of all the noise, Alice felt no one would mind if she went right on in. So she did. The door led into a large kitchen. It was full of smoke. And sitting on a three-legged stool with a baby that looked like a pig was the Duchess herself. A cook was leaning over a cauldron full of soup. A large cat lay on the hearth and grinned from ear to ear.

"There's certainly too much pepper in that soup!" said Alice, sneezing fitfully.

There was too much pepper in the *air*, too. That explained all the sneezing Alice had heard from outside. Even the Duchess sneezed occasionally, and the baby she held in her arms was sneezing *and* bawling. Only the cook and the cat were unaffected.

"Excuse me, please," said Alice, "could you tell me why your cat grins like that?"

"He's a Cheshire Cat," said the Duchess. "That's why. Pig!"

Alice was shocked at this last word. Then Alice realized the Duchess was speaking to the baby, *not* her.

"I didn't know cats could grin," said Alice.

"They all can," said the Duchess, "and most do."

"I don't know of any that do," Alice said politely.

"You don't know much," said the Duchess rudely, "and that's a fact."

Alice was stung by this remark. But what really took her by surprise was the cook's actions. Without warning, the cook removed the cauldron of soup from the fire and began throwing everything within reach at the Duchess and the baby. Fire irons, saucepans, plates, and dishes whizzed through the kitchen air. Some even hit the Duchess, who didn't seem to mind. And it was hard to say whether any hit the baby, who was crying as loudly as ever.

''Watch what you're doing!'' shrieked Alice at the cook. But the cook ignored her and continued chucking things. ''Goodness, what a strange household you have here!''

'' 'Hold,' did you say?'' asked the Duchess, her eyebrows rising. ''Fine. You hold the baby. I must get ready to play croquet with the Queen.'' The Duchess flung the baby at Alice and marched off.

Cradling the baby pig in her arms, Alice walked out of the smoky, peppery kitchen and through the front door. ''If I don't take this baby away with me,'' Alice told herself, ''they're sure to kill it in a day or two.'' The baby grunted and snorted. ''*Shhh!*'' said Alice. ''That's no way to express yourself.''

But the baby grunted and snorted some more. It squirmed in Alice's arms so violently that she had to put it down on the ground. Like a shot, it ran off into the woods—on all fours. Just as well, thought Alice. It would have made a dreadfully ugly child. But it'll make a rather handsome pig, I should think.

As she watched the pig dash into the woods, Alice noticed the Cheshire Cat sitting on a bough of a tree just a few yards away. As usual, the Cat was wearing an ear-to-ear grin, revealing a great many teeth.

"Cheshire Cat," Alice began shyly, "could you tell me, please, which way I ought to go from here?"

"That depends a good deal on where you want to get to," said the Cat.

"I don't much care where— "

"Then it doesn't matter which way you go," interrupted the Cat.

" —so long as I get *somewhere*," said Alice, finishing.

"Oh, you're sure to do that," said the Cat. "Anywhere you go will be somewhere other than here."

"What sort of people live around here?" asked Alice.

"In *that* direction," said the Cat, swinging his right paw around, "lives a Hatter. And in *that* direction," continued the Cat, waving his left paw around, "lives a March Hare. You can visit either one. They're both mad."

"How do you know they're mad?" asked Alice.

"Because we're all mad here. I'm mad. You're mad. They're mad."

"Why do you say I'm mad?"

"You must be," said the Cat. "Otherwise, you wouldn't have come here."

"And how do you know *you're* mad?" asked Alice. Never in her life had she met such creatures. They were all nearly impossible to deal with.

"Is a dog mad?" asked the Cat.

"I suppose not," replied Alice.

"All right, then," said the Cat. "A dog growls when it's angry, and wags its tail when it's happy. *I* growl when I'm happy, and wag my tail when I'm angry. So I must be mad."

Alice was beginning to wonder if the Cat's grin was his way of laughing at her. Then he spoke again. "Are you going to play croquet with the Queen today?"

"I should like to very much," answered Alice. "But I haven't been invited yet."

"You'll see me there," said the Cheshire Cat. Then the strangest thing happened. The Cat started to vanish. From the end of his tail right to his face, the Cat slowly disappeared. Soon only his grin remained. Well, thought Alice, I've often seen a cat without a grin. But I've never seen a grin without a cat!

Alice headed in the direction where the March Hare lived. Before long, she was standing a short distance from a large house. Alice felt sure she was at the right place. The house had chimneys shaped like rabbit ears and a roof thatched with fur.

Alice nibbled on the piece of left-hand mushroom she still had with her. She grew to two feet tall. Then she walked closer to the house. In front of it was a large table where the March Hare and the Hatter were having tea. Between them sat a Dormouse, fast asleep. The other two were using the Dormouse as a kind of cushion, resting their elbows on him.

"No room! No room!" the Hatter and the March Hare cried out when they saw Alice coming near.

"Nonsense!" said Alice. "There's plenty of room."

Indeed there was. The Hatter, March Hare, and Dormouse were all crowded at one corner of the table. The rest of the chairs were empty, and Alice sat in one.

"Have some wine," the March Hare said to Alice in a neighborly tone.

Alice looked all around the table, but there was nothing on it but tea and bread. "I don't see any wine," she said.

"There isn't any," said the March Hare.

"Then it wasn't very nice of you to offer it," Alice said curtly.

"It wasn't very nice of you to sit down without being invited," said the March Hare.

"I didn't know it was *your* table," said Alice. "It's laid out for a great many more than three."

"Your hair needs cutting," said the March Hare.

"And your manners need improving," snapped Alice. "It's very rude to make personal remarks, you know."

"Huh," said the March Hare, unfazed. "Why is a raven like a writing desk?"

At home, Alice always enjoyed riddles. She thought this was the March Hare's way of being friendly. "I believe I can guess that."

"Do you mean that you think you can find out the answer to it?" asked the March Hare.

"Exactly," said Alice.

"Then you should say what you mean," said the March Hare.

"I do," said Alice, flustered. "At least, I mean what I say. That's the same thing, you know."

"Not at all!" said the Hatter. "Why, you might just as well say 'I see what I eat' as 'I eat what I see.'"

"Or 'I like what I get' as 'I get what I like,'" added the March Hare.

"Or 'I breathe when I sleep' is the same thing as 'I sleep when I breathe,'" uttered the Dormouse drowsily.

"It *is* the same thing for you!" the Hatter said to the Dormouse.

Everyone was silent. The only sound was that of the Dormouse's light snoring. Alice was trying to remember how the whole conversation began.

"The Dormouse is asleep again," said the Hatter. He poured some hot tea on the Dormouse's nose. Without ever opening his eyes, the Dormouse wiggled his nose and said, "Of course! Of course! Just what I was going to say myself!"

"Have you guessed the riddle yet?" the Hatter asked Alice.

"Oh, yes, the riddle!" said Alice. "Um, no. What's the answer?"

"I haven't the slightest idea," said the Hatter.

"Nor I," added the March Hare.

Alice's patience had worn out. "I really think you can do something better with your time than ask riddles that have no answers."

"We do! We do!" said the March Hare. "We drink tea! Care for some more?"

"I've had nothing yet," replied Alice coldly, "so I can't take more."

"You mean you can't take *less*," said the Hatter. "It's very easy to take *more* than nothing."

"Nobody asked *your* opinion," said Alice.

"Who's making personal remarks now?" asked the Hatter, almost taunting her.

Alice felt if she didn't leave right that second, she'd explode in anger at the Hatter and March Hare. She got up from the table and walked off. Glancing back over her shoulder, Alice saw the March Hare and the Hatter trying to stuff the still sleeping Dormouse into the teapot. "That was the silliest tea party I've ever been at!" she muttered to herself.

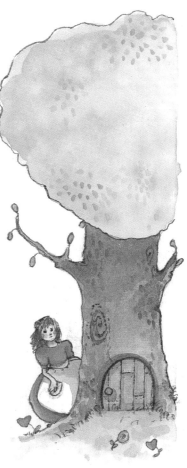

Walking through the woods again, Alice noticed a tree with a door cut into it. That's odd, she thought. But everything's odd in this Wonderland. I might as well enter the door. And she did.

To her surprise, Alice was once more in the long hall with the glass table and the door behind the curtain. The golden key was still on the table, and this time Alice knew what to do. She picked up the key and chewed some of the right-hand mushroom. Alice shrank to a foot in height. Then she unlocked the door, walked down a short passageway, and entered a beautiful garden. She had finally made it!

No sooner had Alice stepped into the garden than she saw three gardeners busily painting a white rosebush red. What was even stranger than that was the gardeners themselves. They were cards—real, honest-to-goodness playing cards! They were Two, Five, and Seven.

"Pardon me," said Alice, "but why are you painting these white roses red?"

Five and Seven looked at Two, who spoke up slowly. "Uh, you see, Miss, this should have been a red rosebush. But by mistake, we planted a white one. If the Queen ever found out, we'd lose our heads for sure. That's why we're doing our best now to—"

"The Queen!" shouted Five, cutting Two off in midsentence. "It's the Queen!" All three gardeners instantly threw themselves face down on the ground.

Alice turned around and saw a whole procession heading toward her. Alice was still standing when the procession stopped beside her. The Queen of Hearts looked at Alice and then asked the Knave of Hearts, "Who's this?" The Knave of Hearts didn't say anything but bowed and smiled.

"Idiot!" said the Queen to the Knave of Hearts. Then she looked straight at Alice. "What's your name, child?"

"My name is Alice, Your Majesty."

"And who are these?" asked the Queen, pointing to the three cards sprawled on the ground. Face down, they looked like all the other cards.

"How should I know?" blurted Alice, surprised at her own courage. "It's no business of mine."

The Queen was outraged. "Off with her head! Off with— "

"Nonsense!" said Alice, loud and defiant.

The Queen hushed up. But the red color in her cheeks showed she was still angry. The King placed his hand on her arm and whispered, "Consider, my dear, she's but a child."

Pulling away from the King's hand, the Queen ordered the Knave of Hearts to turn the three cards over on their backs. The Knave obeyed, and the Queen saw that they were her three gardeners.

"May it please Your Majesty," said Two, his voice trembling as he climbed to his feet, "we were just trying to— "

"Aha!" exclaimed the Queen, seeing the red paint dripping from the white rosebush. "Off with their heads!" Then she moved on with the rest of the procession.

Three soldiers drifted back to behead the three gardeners. But thinking fast, Alice put Two, Five, and Seven into a large flowerpot. The soldiers looked everywhere but in the flowerpot. After a while, they gave up and reported back to the Queen.

"Are their heads off?" she asked them.

"Their heads are gone, Your Majesty!" replied the soldiers truthfully.

"Good!" said the Queen. Then she peeked back at Alice. "Can you play croquet?"

"Yes!" said Alice eagerly.

"Come on, then!" said the Queen.

Alice hurried to join the procession. Walking beside her now was the White Rabbit.

"Where's the Duchess?" asked Alice. "I thought she was supposed to be here to play croquet."

"*Shhh!*" said the Rabbit in a low voice. "The Duchess has been sentenced for beheading."

"What for?" asked Alice in surprise.

"The Duchess arrived later than she should have, and the Queen said— "

"Get to your places!" thundered the Queen.

Everyone scrambled about. After a few moments, the players had taken their positions on the croquet field. Ridges and furrows were all over the playing surface. The croquet balls were live hedgehogs, and the mallets were live flamingos. The wickets were soldiers who stood on their hands and feet, forming arches with their cardboard backs.

The way the game was played was even odder than the field it was played on or the equipment it was played with. No one followed the rules—if there were any. Everyone played out of turn and all at once. Quarreling was constant. Some players fought over the same hedgehogs. And a couple of players used their flamingo mallets to whack each other instead of their hedgehogs. The Queen was in a towering fury the whole time. She stamped about, shouting ''Off with his head!'' or ''Off with her head!'' once a minute. It was total chaos.

With all these beheadings being ordered by the Queen, Alice began to worry. She wondered how long it would take for the Queen to order *her* head removed. Alice tried to stay out of the Queen's way. She also searched for a way to escape. It was then that Alice saw something strange take shape in the air.

Alice watched spellbound for a minute or two. She could now see a grin forming, then whiskers. "It's the Cheshire Cat!" she said in excitement.

"How are you getting along?" asked the Cat as soon as there was mouth enough for him to speak with.

Alice waited for the Cat's ears and entire head to appear before replying. "Not well at all," Alice said to the Cat's head. The rest of his body never appeared. "I was just about to hit my hedgehog through a wicket when the wicket got up and wandered off. And earlier, the Queen's hedgehog ran away when it saw my hedgehog rolling toward it. Besides that, everyone keeps arguing and yelling. It's sheer madness out there!"

"Who *are* you speaking to?" asked the King, who was playing close by.

"Let me introduce a friend of mine, Your Majesty," said Alice. "This is the Cheshire Cat."

"*Hmm,*" said the King, peering up at the head hovering in the air. "Well, it must be removed." He then called out to the Queen. "My dear, I wish you would have this Cat removed."

The Queen came over and immediately said, "Off with his head! Off with his head!"

"I'll get the executioner myself, dear," said the King, hurrying away.

When the King returned with the executioner, an argument broke out. The executioner told the King and Queen that he couldn't cut off a head unless there was a body to cut it off from. The King argued that anything that had a head could be beheaded. The Queen argued that if something wasn't done about it quickly, she'd have *everybody* executed.

"The Cat belongs to the Duchess," mentioned Alice. "Maybe she could help."

"Yes," said the Queen. She turned to the executioner. "Fetch her from prison."

The executioner left to get the Duchess. But by the time he came back with her, the Cheshire Cat's head had faded completely away.

With nothing else to do, the King and Queen resumed their croquet game. The Duchess slowly walked over to the Queen, curtsied, and said in a weak voice, "A fine day, Your Majesty."

The Queen, lining up her next croquet shot, stared at the Duchess menacingly. "I give you fair warning," shouted the Queen, stamping her foot. "Either you or your head must be off! Take your pick! And be quick about it!" The Queen barely finished her words before the Duchess curtsied again and bolted away.

The Queen looked over at Alice now. "Have you seen the Mock Turtle yet?"

"No," answered Alice. "I don't even know what a Mock Turtle is."

"Silly girl," said the Queen. "It's the thing Mock Turtle Soup is made from." The Queen grabbed Alice's hand and pulled her along. "I'll let him tell you his story."

The Queen took Alice to where a Gryphon stood sunning himself by the sea. "Take her to see the Mock Turtle!" commanded the Queen. She turned and left Alice alone with the Gryphon. He was a strange creature, having the head and wings of an eagle and the body of a lion. The Gryphon led Alice to the Mock Turtle, who was sobbing on a little ledge of rock.

"What's the matter with you?" Alice asked the Mock Turtle.

Dabbing the tears from his eyes, the Mock Turtle said, "Sit down, both of you, and I'll tell you." When Alice and the Gryphon were seated, the Mock Turtle began. "Once, I was a *real* turtle. And as a very young turtle, I went to school in the sea. The teacher was an old turtle. We used to call him Tortoise."

"Why did you call him Tortoise if he wasn't one?" asked Alice.

"We called him Tortoise because he taught us," said the Mock Turtle, annoyed at the interruption. Then he continued. "We learned all the usual lessons—reeling and writhing and so on."

"And how many hours a day did you do lessons?" asked Alice.

"Ten hours the first day," replied the Mock Turtle. "Nine hours the next day, eight hours the next, and so on."

"That's strange," said Alice.

"Not at all," said the Mock Turtle. "That's the reason they're called lessons—because they lessen from day to day."

"Then the eleventh day must have been a holiday," said Alice, computing in her head.

"Of course," said the Mock Turtle.

"But how did you manage on the twelfth day?" asked Alice.

"That's enough about lessons," broke in the Gryphon. "Tell her about the Lobster Quadrille."

"What's that?" asked Alice. She was having trouble understanding everything that was being said. But then, nearly every creature she'd met so far in Wonderland was hard to understand.

"It's a dance," said the Mock Turtle. "You get into two lines. One line is made up of seals, turtles, and salmon. The other line is their partners—all lobsters. You move forward by two steps, change lobsters, and move back two steps. Then you throw the lobsters out to sea, swim out after them, do a somersault in the water, and swim back with them to shore. Sometimes you can do the Lobster Quadrille with a porpoise. In fact, most won't do anything without a porpoise."

"Don't you mean 'purpose'?" asked Alice.

"I mean what I say," snapped the Mock Turtle.

Alice was about to argue with him when suddenly a voice shouted from the distance, "The trial's about to begin at the royal court!"

"Come on!" said the Gryphon. He took Alice by the hand, and the two left the Mock Turtle standing on the rock ledge. He never did get to finish his story.

When Alice and the Gryphon arrived at the royal court, the King and Queen of Hearts were seated on their throne. A great crowd had gathered in front of them. There were birds and beasts of all descriptions, as well as a whole pack of cards. Standing between two soldiers was the Knave of Hearts, bound in chains. A table with a large dish of tarts on it was in the middle of the court.

The King acted as judge, and twelve birds and beasts sitting in a wooden box were the jury. Alice saw the jury writing on slates and asked the Gryphon what they were doing. "They're writing their names down in case they forget them," the Gryphon whispered to Alice.

"Stupid things!" said Alice in too loud a voice.

"Silence in the court!" shouted the White Rabbit, who stepped up beside the King and Queen.

Alice glanced over at the jury box again. She saw them writing "Stupid things!" on their slates.

"Read the charge!" ordered the King.

The White Rabbit unfurled a scroll and read:

> *The Queen of Hearts, she made some tarts,*
> *All on a summer day;*
> *The Knave of Hearts, he stole those tarts,*
> *And took them quite away.*

"Let the first witness come forward!" commanded the King.

Approaching the throne was the Hatter. He had a teacup in one hand and a slice of buttered bread in the other hand. Right behind him walked the March Hare and the Dormouse. They found two empty seats and sat down.

"Take off your hat!" the King said to the Hatter.

"It isn't mine, Your Majesty," said the Hatter.

"Aha! *Stolen!*" the King exclaimed. He looked over at the jury, who immediately wrote down his words on their slates.

"I keep them to sell," the Hatter said in his own defense. "I've none of my own. I'm a hatter, you see."

"Never mind," said the King. "Give your evidence. And don't be nervous—or I'll have you beheaded on the spot!"

The Hatter *was* nervous, however. He kept shifting from one foot to the other. Alice felt sorry for him. But suddenly *she* felt uneasy. Oh, my, thought Alice. I'm beginning to grow large again!

"Your Majesty," said the Hatter, "I'm a poor man. My bread and butter were getting thin, and the twinkling of the tea— "

"The twinkling of *what?*" interrupted the King.

"Actually, it began with the tea," replied the Hatter.

"I know 'twinkling' *begins* with a T!" roared the King. "Do you take me for an idiot? Go on!"

"I'm a poor man," continued the Hatter, "and the tea started to twinkle. At least, the March Hare said— "

"I didn't!" shouted the March Hare from his seat.

"You did!" said the Hatter.

"I deny it!" said the March Hare.

"He denies it," said the King, looking over at the jury. "Leave that part out."

Alice, still growing bigger, leaned over to the Gryphon and asked, "*What* part?"

The Gryphon told Alice to be quiet and watch.

"I'm a poor man," the Hatter said again to the King.

"You're a very poor speaker!" said the King. And once more, the jury wrote down his words.

Alice soon became bored with the trial. Even when the Duchess' cook was called as a witness and told her story about pepper, Alice lost interest. She snapped to, however, when the next witness was called.

"Alice!" read the White Rabbit from his scroll.

Startled to hear her name, Alice jumped up. But she had grown so large by now that she upended the jury box near her. All the birds and beasts toppled out onto the floor. Alice apologized, then picked them up and put them back in the jury box. Right away, the jury started writing a history of the accident on their slates.

"What do you know about this business?" the King asked Alice, now standing before him.

"Nothing," replied Alice.

"Nothing *whatever?*" asked the King.

"Nothing whatever," answered Alice.

"That's *very* important," the King told the jury, who wrote it down.

"*Ahem,*" said the White Rabbit, as if clearing his throat. "I believe Your Majesty meant *un*important."

"Quite right," said the King. "Unimportant it is!" He glanced over at the jury. "And that's important to know!" The jury scribbled on their slates again. Then the King turned his gaze back to Alice. "You've broken Rule Forty-Two: 'All persons more than a mile high must leave the court.'"

"But I'm not a mile high," said Alice.

"You are," said the King.

"Nearly *two* miles high," added the Queen.

"Nonsense!" said Alice. "You just made that rule up."

"It's the oldest rule in the book," said the King.

"Then it ought to be number one, *not* forty-two," said Alice.

The King was silent for a minute, then looked over at the jury. "Have you reached your verdict?" he asked.

"No, no!" said the Queen, very upset. "Sentence first— verdict afterward."

"What?" said Alice. "Whoever heard of a sentence coming before a verdict?"

"Hold your tongue!" commanded the Queen, her face purple with rage.

"I won't!" said Alice, angry herself.

"Off with her head!" yelled the Queen. "Off with her head!"

"Oh, phooey!" Alice shouted back. "You're nothing but a pack of cards!"

Suddenly, the whole pack rose up in the air and came flying down on her. Alice screamed. Instinctively, she protected her eyes and face with one arm. Alice flailed her other arm, trying to keep the cards off her.

"*Ouch!*"

Who said that? wondered Alice. Slowly, she removed the arm covering her eyes. In the sunlight above, the face of Alice's older sister stared down at her. She was rubbing her cheek.

"Wake up, Alice! Wake up!" said her sister. "That must have been some dream you were having! You were swinging your arm wildly. You even hit me in the face."

"Oh, I'm sorry," said Alice, sitting up now on the river-bank. "I didn't mean it. It's just that I had the *strangest* dream you could ever imagine!"

"I'm sure it was, Alice dear," said her sister. "And you can tell me all about it later. Right now, you had better scoot home for tea. You're late."

Nodding, Alice got up, brushed the leaves off her dress, and raced home. The wind whooshed through her hair as she ran. Is there a Wonderland—somewhere? Alice didn't know.

Even at home, drinking her tea, Alice asked herself the same question. But as she poured more tea into her cup, Alice started to giggle. In her mind, she could still see the March Hare and Hatter trying to stuff the dozing Dormouse into a teapot.